Angela Nicely

Queen Bee!

ALAN MACDONALD ILLUSTRATED BY **DAVID ROBERTS**

Look out for the
next *Angela Nicely*
book, coming soon:
Superstar!

Have you read the first
Angela Nicely book?

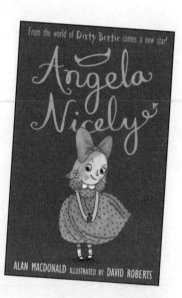

Contents

1   Matchmaker!   7

2   The Big Bike Ride!   37

3   The Ugly Sisters!   69

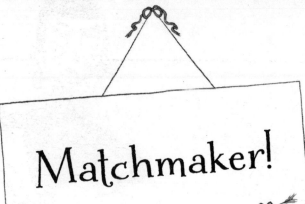

Matchmaker!

Chapter 1

"ANGELA NICELY!" cried Miss Darling. "Are you talking?"

"No, only whispering," said Angela.

"That's the same thing," said Miss Darling. "When I say work quietly I mean QUIETLY!"

Angela jumped. Miss Darling was certainly in a crabby mood today.

She'd already shouted at Maisie and snapped at Kevin for drawing on his face. Her eyes were red and she kept reaching for her hanky. Maybe she'd stayed up past her bedtime last night.

Angela noticed a magazine poking out of her teacher's bag. She squinted, trying to read the headline in red letters.

Angela sat up. That was it! That explained Miss Darling's bad mood. She'd been dumped by her boyfriend! Wait till she told Maisie and Laura. Angela was an expert on boyfriend trouble. She had split up with Bertie hundreds of times, although according to him they were never going out.

At break time Angela called an emergency meeting of the GOBS club (Girls Only, Boys Smell).

"Is everyone here?" she said.

"You can see we're here," sighed Maisie.

"Good, because we've got to do something about Miss Darling," said Angela. "She's been dumped by her boyfriend."

Laura gasped. "How do you know?"

"It's so obvious!" said Angela. "She's all moody, and you can tell she's been crying."

"So? I don't see what we can do," said Maisie.

Angela gave her a look. "Well, DUH!" she said. "We can find her a new boyfriend!"

The other two stared. It was a brilliant idea. After all, Miss Darling *deserved* a nice boyfriend.

"Okay, but who?" said Maisie.

Angela frowned. The fact was, boyfriends weren't exactly growing on trees. There was Bertie, of course, but he was Angela's boyfriend and anyway he picked his nose. Besides, it needed to be someone nearer Miss Darling's age – about twenty-one or forty.

'There's Mr Grouch," she said.

'The caretaker? He's ancient!" cried Maisie.

"And bald *and* grumpy," added Laura.

Angela had to admit Mr Grouch wasn't a dream come true – he was more of a nightmare. But that only left one person.

'Then it'll have to be Mr Weakly," she said.

"MR WEAKLY?" squawked Laura. "Who'd want to go out with *him*?"

Mr Weakly was the only male teacher at the school. He was pale, nervous and hid behind a pair of thick glasses. Still, he was their only hope.

"He's just a bit shy," said Angela.

"Shy?" said Maisie. "He goes bright red if you ask a question! Can you imagine him asking Miss Darling out?"

Angela sighed. It was easier to imagine Mr Weakly becoming a lion tamer.

"Okay then, we'll just have to give him some tips!" she said.

Miss Darling was going to get a boyfriend even if it took all year. Angela was sure she'd be grateful. One day she might even need a bridesmaid…

Chapter 2

At lunchtime the GOBS club found a
quiet corner of the playground. Angela
took out a pen and paper.

"So what shall we write?" she asked.

"Oh, Miss Darling! I LOVE you!
I want to MARRY you!" sighed Laura,
clutching her heart.

"No," said Maisie firmly. "It's got to

be like one of those romantic cards."

"Valentine's cards you mean," said Angela.

She had seen the card her mum got on Valentine's Day. It had a large pink heart on the front and a soppy poem inside. It couldn't be that difficult. She began to write.

Oh deer luvly Miss D
I think your pritty as a pea
Yor eyes are blu, yor smyle is twinkly
Yor face is pink and not too wrinkly.
Evry day wen you walk by
I feel so sik I want to cry,
So come at four and I will wate
In the staff room - don't be late!

Now for Mr Weakly. Angela took a
fresh piece of paper. She was getting
pretty good at this.

> Mr Weakly, Mr Weakly,
> Peeple say yor nose is beuky
> And yor face all payl and spotty
> Makes you look compleetly potty!
> But if I cud make a wish
> You wood be my faverit dish.
> So come at four and say yor mine
> In the staff room - be on time!

"That should do it," said Angela.
"Now we just need someone to deliver
the letters."

"Don't look at me, it's your idea," said
Maisie.

"I've done all the writing," said Angela.

"Laura can take them."

"ME? Why me?" grumbled Laura.

"You're the smallest," said Angela. "You won't get seen."

Laura sniffed, putting on her coat. "Well, I don't see why I should take them both. Maisie isn't doing *anything*!"

Angela sighed. It was hard work being leader of the GOBS club. She had to organize everything.

"Okay, me and Maisie will take Mr Weakly's then," she said. "He's going to need our help anyway."

Laura put Miss Darling's letter in her pocket. She wondered what Angela meant by "help" exactly.

Chapter 3

Laura crossed the playground. Wait, there was Miss Darling, talking to Miss Boot on a bench! This was her chance. If she crept up quietly the teachers would be too busy chatting to notice her. But what if they turned round? She needed a disguise, just in case. Laura took off her coat and put it on back to front. With the hood up no one would recognize her.

The only drawback was that she couldn't see where she was going. She set off in the direction of the bench with her hands outstretched.

"Ugh! This hayfever!" Miss Darling was grumbling to Miss Boot. "My eyes won't stop…"

CRASH!

"What on earth?" cried Miss Boot, swinging round.

Laura pulled down her hood and blinked.

"Ouch! Sorry, Miss," she said. "I couldn't see where I was going."

"I'm not surprised with your coat over your head," sniffed Miss Darling.

"Sometimes I despair," said Miss Boot. "Well, is there something you wanted, Laura?"

"Um… No Miss."

Laura turned to go. But the letter was still in her pocket and Angela would go mad if she didn't deliver it.

She stooped down, pretending to tie her laces. No one was looking. She slipped the letter under the bench by Miss Darling's feet. She was bound to see it when she got up. Operation Lovebirds was up and running.

Meanwhile, Maisie and Angela had tracked Mr Weakly down to his classroom. They knocked on the door.

"Come in!" Mr Weakly looked up from a pile of books.

Angela smiled innocently. "Sir, can I ask you a question?"

"Er, yes, if you must," said Mr Weakly.

"Have you got a girlfriend?"

Mr Weakly gulped and blushed all the way up to his ears.

"Um... Well..." he stammered. "I can't say, um... No, not really."

"Maybe it'd help if you were a bit more, like, trendy," said Maisie.

"Yes," agreed Angela. "If you wore jeans, and trainers instead of sandals."

"Ha ha! Yes, you could be right!" said Mr Weakly.

"I know," cried Angela. "Take off your glasses!"

"But... but I won't be able to see."

"Try it, sir," said Maisie.

Mr Weakly obeyed. He blinked like a newborn chick.

"Much better!" said Angela.

"You look cool," said Maisie.

"Cool?" repeated Mr Weakly. If anything he felt terribly hot.

Angela inspected him. "Hmm," she

said, "but we still need to do something with your hair."

She took out a plastic pot. "Hold still, sir," she said.

Soon Mr Weakly's hair stood up like a spiky hedgehog. Angela admired her work. It was amazing what you could do with a pot of glue.

"Wow! You look like a film star!" she said.

"Like James Bond," agreed Maisie. "Take a look, sir."

They led him over to the mirror inside the cupboard door. Mr Weakly blinked. He hardly knew himself – mainly because he was blind as a bat without his glasses.

He cleared his throat.

"You really think…?"

"I bet you could get any girlfriend you want," said Angela. "I bet they'll be dying to go out with you."

Mr Weakly squinted at his reflection. Maybe they were right! Without his glasses, he looked different – taller, more handsome, less spotty. He attempted a devilish smile.

When he turned back Angela was holding up a scrap of paper.

23

"Oh, we found this," said Angela. "Someone must have slipped it under the door."

Mr Weakly took the letter and fumbled for his glasses. As he read his eyes grew bigger. This was amazing – incredible! He had a secret admirer! But who? Mrs Trump? Miss Skinner? Or maybe nice Miss Darling? His heart raced. He'd almost spoken to her once at a staff meeting. Four o'clock – he'd make sure to be there on the dot!

Back in the playground, the bell had just gone. Miss Darling wiped her runny nose and hurried back into school. Miss Boot got to her feet.

"LINE UP! NO TALKING!" she barked.

Wait, what was this under the bench? Miss Boot unfolded a letter. She gasped. Her glasses steamed up. Good gravy! Someone had written her a poem! It mentioned her twinkly smile, her blue eyes… Clearly the writer was colour blind and couldn't spell. But who could have written it? There was only one way to find out. At four o'clock she would be in the staff room waiting!

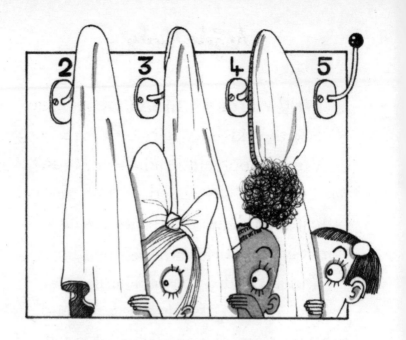

Chapter 4

DRRRRRING! The bell rang for the end of school.

Angela, Laura and Maisie hid in the cloakroom until everyone had gone home. When the coast was clear they hurried to the staff room. It was ten to four – almost time for the big date.

Angela peeped through the keyhole.

"Well! Are they in there?" asked Maisie.

"Are they kissing?" giggled Laura.

Angela shook her head. "Shh! I can't see anything," she hissed.

Just then they heard footsteps coming down the hall.

"Quick! Hide!" hissed Maisie.

They dashed round the corner and crouched out of sight. Angela poked out her head and saw Mr Weakly arrive.

His hair stood strangely on end as if he was a human paintbrush. He had loosened his tie and was smiling a sickly smile. Taking off his glasses, he fumbled for the door handle and went in.

Angela and her friends crept out to listen at the door. Mr Weakly would be sitting next to Miss Darling now. They would be holding hands and whispering sweet nothings to each other. Angela wished they would speak up a bit because she couldn't hear a peep.

Inside, Mr Weakly stood with his back to the door. He had turned even paler than usual. The person waiting for him was not sweet Miss Darling – it was scary Miss Boot.

"Mr Weakly!" she said, jumping to her feet.

"Oh! Ah! Miss Boot!" gulped Mr Weakly. "I wasn't … um… What are *you* doing here?"

Miss Boot gave a girlish laugh. "Ha, ha, you silly boy! Don't pretend you don't know! Oh…" Mr Weakly noticed her staring at his hair.

"Oh, ah yes… it's sort of new," he said, going pink.

Miss Boot sat down, patting the sofa beside her.

"Well, I came as you asked," she smiled.

"Me?"

"Yes, in your letter."

Mr Weakly looked blank. "What letter? *You* wrote to *me*."

"Don't be ridiculous!" snapped Miss Boot. "Do you deny you asked me to come at four o'clock?"

"Um no… Yes!" squeaked Mr Weakly, starting to sweat. "I mean you told *me* to come."

Miss Boot glared. "I *certainly* did not!"

"But it's in your letter," said Mr Weakly, pulling it from his pocket.

Miss Boot read the scrawl. It was the same handwriting and hopeless spelling. Something funny was going on, and she meant to get to the bottom of it.

Outside, Angela, Laura and Maisie listened at the door. They could hear muffled voices but couldn't make out the words.

"It sounds like they're arguing," said Maisie.

Angela nodded. "That means they're in love."

Laura sighed. "I wish we could see what's going on."

Angela put her ear to the door again. Now it had gone quiet. Maybe if she opened the door just a crack she could peep inside. She turned the door handle...

"ANGELA NICELY!"

Angela was so surprised that she fell into the room. She looked round to see

31

Miss Darling standing over her. But if Miss Darling was there, who'd been talking to Mr Weakly?

"WHAT ON EARTH IS GOING ON?" barked a voice.

Uh oh, thought Angela.

"Good question, Miss Boot," said Miss Darling. "I found these three girls listening at the door."

Maisie and Laura shuffled into the room.

Miss Boot waved a piece of paper.

"Someone has been sending me letters!" she said.

Angela sat up. "YOU?"

"That's what I said."

"But the letter wasn't for *you*, it was meant for Miss Darling!"

Angela clapped a hand over her mouth, but it was too late. Miss Boot's face looked like thunder.

"So YOU wrote it, did you?" she boomed.

Mr Weakly sat down, feeling faint.

Miss Darling read the letter he'd dropped.

"I think you have some explaining to do, Angela," she said.

"I was only trying to help!" cried Angela. "I saw you'd been crying so I thought a new boyfriend would cheer you up."

Miss Darling raised her eyes to heaven. "I hadn't been crying. I've got hayfever, Angela. What I need is a day off!"

Angela stared at her feet. "Oh," she said, backing towards the door. Maybe it was time to go.

"BACK HERE!" barked Miss Boot. "Since you're so fond of writing you can get in some practice. One hundred lines on my desk by tomorrow!"

Angela threw up her hands. Honestly, some people were *so ungrateful!*

The Big
Bike Ride!

Chapter 1

It was Saturday. Angela bounded into the kitchen and grabbed her dad round the waist.

"What's all this?" he asked.

"Pocket money day!" cried Angela.

"Ah, I might have known," laughed Mr Nicely. "How much did we agree?"

"A THOUSAND POUNDS!" yelled

Angela at the top of her voice.

"Ha ha!" said Dad. "One pound fifty, I think."

He placed the coins in Angela's hand.

She whooped, dancing around the kitchen. "YAHOO! I'm rich! I'm rich! I'm… EH?" The money was snatched from her hand.

"We'll put that in your moneybox," said Mrs Nicely, appearing from nowhere.

"But I need it!" wailed Angela.

"Sensible children save their pocket money," said Mrs Nicely.

"Couldn't I just spend a bit?" pleaded Angela. "Laura and Maisie are going to the sweet shop."

"Surely a few sweets can't do any harm," said her dad.

"Sweets are bad for your teeth," frowned Mrs Nicely, dropping the coins into Angela's moneybox.

Later Maisie and Laura called round and they all walked to the sweet shop on the corner. Angela sighed. It was so unfair. Maisie and Laura would be buying

39

sackfuls of sweets while she couldn't even afford one measly jellybean. Wait a moment, though – maybe she could *earn* some money?

"Laura, did you brush your hair today?" she asked.

"Yes," said Laura. "Why?"

"Oh, it just looks a bit boring," said Angela.

Laura pouted. "ANGELA! YOU ARE SO MEAN!"

"I'm only trying to help," said Angela. "It could be fair like mine – or even pink. I can colour it."

"Laura's hair is nice as it is," said Maisie.

"At the hairdressers it costs thousands," said Angela. "But I'll do it for a pound."

"No, thank you," said Laura.

"Eighty pence?" said Angela.

"ANGELA!" cried Maisie. "Just 'cos you haven't got any money!"

Angela sighed. Maisie and Laura were her best friends, but sometimes they could be very selfish. Where could she lay her hands on some sweetie money? She stopped suddenly. On a lamppost was a large sign.

THE WHEELY BIG BIKE RIDE

COMING SOON!
Sunday 14th June

"Sunday?" said Angela. "Isn't that tomorrow?"

"Of course. The bike ride is going down your road," said Maisie.

"Mine?" said Angela.

She half remembered her dad saying something about a charity bike ride. Wasn't he in training? That's why he kept coming in wearing tight shorts that made his bottom look big and bulgy.

Angela's eyes lit up. A bike ride coming down her road? This was perfect – they could set up a stall. Cyclists meant customers – and customers had money to spend!

But what would cyclists want to buy? Stabilizers? Plasters? Bubble gum? No...

"DRINKS!" cried Angela. "We could sell lemonade!"

Laura and Maisie looked at her in surprise.

"What for?" said Laura.

"For money, pea brain!" said Angela. "Cycling makes you thirsty. We'll earn a fortune!"

Maisie rolled her eyes. "But Angela we don't *have* any lemonade."

"Not yet we don't!" said Angela.

Chapter 2

Once the sweets were gone they set to work in the kitchen.

Angela put on her apron. "Now," she said. "What do we need to make lemonade?"

"Lemon," said Maisie.

"And Ade," said Laura.

"Ade is the fizzy bit," said Maisie.

"How do you make it fizzy?" asked Laura.

Angela thought hard. You could blow bubbles through a straw, but they wouldn't last long.

Wait – what about her mum's private stash of fizzy water? Angela wasn't allowed to drink it because it "cost the earth". But that was okay because *she* wasn't going to drink it.

She found some lemons and put them in the washing-up bowl.

Angela bashed them using a rolling pin.

BANG!

WHACK!

THUMP!

They examined the flattened lemons.

"Hmm. Don't we just need the juice?" asked Maisie.

Angela shook her head. "Leave the lemons in. It all adds to the taste," she said.

Next they poured in three bottles of Highland Breeze Sparkling Water. GLUG, GLUG, GLUG!

Angela stirred the mixture with a spoon. Quite a bit splashed on her clothes and some slopped on the floor. She tried a spoonful. "EWW! Not sweet enough!" she cried, pulling a face.

"Sugar," said Maisie.

Angela poured in a bag of sugar, although half of it went on the floor. She splish-sploshed with her spoon again and tested a mouthful.

"Perfect!" she cried, licking sugar from her lips.

"It's rather bitty," said Maisie.

"It's *s'posed* to be bitty," said Angela.

"But shouldn't there be more bubbles?" asked Laura.

"Shake it up, that'll make it fizzy," Angela suggested. She found a plastic bottle and poured in the sugary liquid.

GLOOP, GLOOP, GLOOP!

Lemonade gushed down the sides of the bottle, spilling on to the floor.

Angela screwed on the top and shook the bottle hard.

WHOOSH!

Suddenly the cap flew off and lemonade spurted everywhere.

"ARGHH!" screamed Angela. "MAKE IT STOP!"

Mrs Nicely heard the noise and came rushing in. "What on earth…?"

She stared in horror. Her kitchen looked like it had been hit by a hurricane. Drawers lay open, there was sugar everywhere and the floor was swimming in puddles. Angela was clutching a bottle, which was frothing all over her dress.

"ANGELA!" yelled her mum. "I hope that isn't my Highland Breeze Sparkling Water?"

Angela gulped. "It wasn't my fault," she said.

Once they'd cleared up the mess, Angela tried to explain.

Mrs Nicely folded her arms. "You want to sell lemonade on the street?" she asked.

"Not on the street – in our garden!" said Angela.

"Yes, but who to?"

"To the cyclers," said Angela. "You know – like Dad."

Mrs Nicely remembered. Tomorrow was the big bike ride that passed down their road. Her husband was taking part.

"Don't you need permission to sell drinks?" she said. "And where's the money going?"

Angela looked at her feet. "Er, well … actually…"

"We're giving it to charity!" cried Maisie.

Angela looked surprised.

"You know, poor people," said Maisie, nodding.

Mrs Nicely's expression softened. "Oh well, if it's for charity that's different," she beamed. "But if you're making lemonade, you'd better do it properly." She went off to find her recipe book.

Angela looked at Maisie.

"*Poor people?*" she said. "What poor people?"

Maisie shrugged. "Well *you're* poor, aren't you? You haven't got any pocket money."

Chapter 3

On Sunday morning, Mrs Nicely
helped them set out cups on a table in
the front garden. Angela had drawn a
big sign:

ARE YOU THURSTY?
SUPA·FIZZEE HOME·MAID
LEMONAID HERE!!
ONLY 50P!

Three big jugs of cold lemonade stood
ready. Mrs Nicely retired to the house
for some peace and quiet.

"I'll be in charge of the money," said Angela.

"And I'll be in charge of drinks, 'cos I'm best at pouring," said Maisie.

"What am I in charge of?" asked Laura.

Angela thought for a moment. "Customers," she said. "You can make sure they all stop at the stand."

It was a warm, sunny day. Soon Angela expected a queue stretching all the way down the road. This was probably her greatest idea ever. How much was thirty times 50p? It was a lot, anyway – enough to buy a hundred fizzy snakes.

They waited. Maisie arranged the cups into neat lines. Angela slurped some lemonade.

"Angela!" cried Maisie.

"What? I'm just checking it's fizzy enough," said Angela. She pulled a face. Maisie could be such a bossy boots sometimes.

ZOOOOOOM!

Suddenly two bikes whizzed past at top speed. Angela looked after them in dismay.

"LAURA! You're meant to STOP them!" Angela complained.

"How?" said Laura.

"I don't know! Wave at them."

Laura sighed. Why couldn't she be the one in charge of drinks instead of Maisie? She trailed down to the gate to watch the road.

Five minutes later a group of cyclists came peddling over the hill.

Laura waved her arms in the air. "HEY! STOP!" she cried. "Would you like…?"

ZOOM! The bikes went whizzing past. Laura turned and shrugged helplessly.

Angela came marching down the garden path. "What are you *doing*?" she sighed.

"I waved," said Laura. "They didn't let me finish!"

"But you have to *make* them stop!" frowned Angela.

"How?" asked Laura. "I can't stand in the road. I'll get run over!"

Angela looked around. There had to be some way to make the cyclists stop. Across the road was a sign on a lamppost. It showed a big green arrow and a picture of a bike.

Hmm, thought Angela, *obviously the cyclists followed the green arrows.* So if an arrow pointed somewhere else – into someone's front garden, for instance – the cyclists would follow the sign.

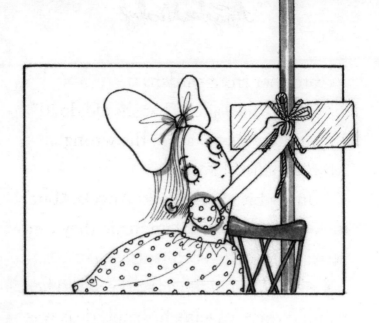

Chapter 4

Angela stood on a chair, untying the sign on the lamppost.

"ANGELA, YOU CAN'T!" cried Laura.

"You'll get us in to trouble!" said Maisie.

"I'm not taking it down, am I?" said Angela. "I'm just moving it a bit." She turned the sign so the arrow pointed

58

towards her front garden.

"There," she said. "That should do it!"

"But now they'll all go the wrong way!" moaned Laura.

"Only a bit wrong," said Angela. "But once they've bought lemonade they can go right again. It's brilliant!"

Laura raised her eyes to the sky. The trouble with Angela's brilliant ideas was that they usually ended in disaster.

A few minutes later another group of cyclists came over the hill. The first rider saw the green arrow and slammed on his brakes.

"Is this sign correct?" he asked, puzzled.

"Well, it says turn right," said his friend. "But right where?"

"'Scuse me," said a voice. "Would you like some lemonade?"

The cyclists turned their heads. A girl with dark hair was pointing them towards a drinks stall.

"It's home-made," said Laura. "With real actual lemons."

Soon there was a queue of a dozen riders at the drink stall. Maisie poured lemonade while Angela took the money, jingling coins in her cash box. More cyclists were arriving every minute. A pile of bikes was propped against a wall.

"That'll be fifty pence, please," said Angela.

A tall, skinny cyclist handed over his money.

"So, whose bright idea was this?" he asked.

"Mine," said Angela, proudly.

"But me and Laura did most of the work," added Maisie quickly.

Angela shot her a sharp look.

"Well, you'll certainly be busy," said the man. "Especially when the rest of them arrive."

Angela nodded. "Are there many more?"

The cyclist laughed. "Many? You're joking! There's hundreds of them."

Just then Laura let out a cry. "Uh oh," she said. "LOOK!"

61

Angela turned and her mouth fell open. Over the hill rose a great sea of bikes – more bikes than she had ever seen in her life. They swept down the road in wave upon wave. If they all stopped, they'd fill Angela's front garden and take up the entire pavement.

They were almost at the sign. Angela covered her eyes, unable to watch. The cyclists who saw the sign tried to turn at the last minute – the rest tried to keep going.

SCREEEEEECH!

CRASH!

When Angela peeped out, cyclists were littering the road. Bikes were piled on top of each other with their pedals and handlebars tangled like knitting.

"Oh dear!" said Laura.

"Oops!" said Angela.

"Now you've done it," said Maisie.

A red-faced steward arrived and waded through the bikes to Angela's front garden.

"What's going on? Who moved this arrow?" he demanded.

One of the cyclists got off his bike and took off his helmet. It was Mr Nicely. "Angela?" he said.

Everyone turned their heads to stare at Angela.

"You! Did you move that sign?" said the steward, crossly.

"Er ... um ..." said Angela.

Luckily, at that moment Mrs Nicely came out of her house. She had heard the deafening crash.

"Who is in charge here?" she scolded. "Get these bikes sorted out! And kindly get your boots off my flower bed!"

The steward backed off, mumbling an apology.

Soon the bikes were untangled and their riders peddling off down the road.

Angela breathed a sigh of relief. Thank goodness for her mum. And at least they still had all the lovely money they'd made! She jingled the coins in the cash box.

"I'll look after that, thank you," said Mrs Nicely, grabbing it.

"But ... but we earned it!" cried Angela.

"Yes, and I'll make it sure it goes to a very good charity," nodded Mrs Nicely. "Well done, girls. Now, don't forget to clear up!"

Angela stared after her mum open-mouthed. Life was *so* unfair!

The Ugly
Sisters

Chapter 1

Angela and Laura were walking to
school. Every morning Mrs Nicely
watched them down the road. They
walked the last part by themselves once
they reached the alley.

"Uh oh," said Laura, as they turned
the corner.

Angela looked up. Two dark figures

guarded the alley – the terrible twins,
Eileen and Myleen.

The Payne twins were the biggest
bullies in Angela's class. They both
had black hair, heavy eyebrows and
evil smiles. Myleen had a hairy mole
above her mouth. Angela called them
the Ugly Sisters – although not to their
faces, of course. But last week she'd
laughed when Eileen leaned too far
back and fell off her chair ... the twins
had sworn revenge.

"Let's go the other way," begged
Laura.

Angela shook her head. "No way. I'm
not scared of *them*."

"Well I am," said Laura. "They're
horrible meanies."

But Angela never backed down. She

kept walking towards the alley.

"Oh look, it's Goldilocks!" teased Myleen. "Where are you off to?"

"School," said Angela. "Come on, Laura."

They tried to push past, but the twins blocked their path.

"Sorry," said Myleen. "This is OUR alley."

"Yeah, we own it," said Eileen, folding her arms. "And *you* can't come through."

"Not unless you pay," nodded Myleen.

Laura tugged at Angela's arm.

"Come on, Angela, let's go back," she whispered.

But Angela hated anyone giving her orders. They always took the alley to school and she didn't see why they should change now.

72

"Let us through," she said.

"Only if you pay up," said Myleen.

Angela rolled her eyes. "I don't have any money."

"What's in your bag?" demanded Eileen.

"Just my lunch," replied Angela.

The twins smirked at each other. Suddenly, Myleen snatched Angela's bag and looked inside. She grabbed the lunch box. "Yum! We like crisps," she said.

The twins also helped themselves to Angela's chocolate bar.

"Give it back!" yelled Angela.

Myleen shook her head. "Like we said, no payment, no entry."

Angela glared. How she wanted to wipe the smile off Myleen's smug face!

But how? There were two of the twins, and Laura was no use at fighting. She burst into tears if someone called her a name.

"Awww, poor Goldilocks. She's hungry!" said Eileen, munching crisps.

"Yeah, let's make her a sandwich," said her sister.

Myleen grabbed one of Angela's sandwiches and threw away the cheese and tomato. She spread a handful of thick brown mud on the bread, and then squished the two slices together.

"There you are, A NICE MUD SANDWICH!" she smirked.

"Your favourite!" cried Eileen. "Eat up, Goldilocks!"

Angela looked at their grinning faces, then at the revolting sandwich. Gloopy

brown mud oozed between the slices
of bread. But she wasn't going to back
down, even now.

Snatching the sandwich, she took a
big bite.

"Scrummy!" she said, with mud
round her mouth.

The twins gawped at her with their mouths open. Angela stuck out her tongue, grabbed her things and marched off down the alley, with Laura hurrying to catch up.

Once the twins were out of sight, Angela stopped and spat out a piece of soggy bread.

"PLUGH! UGH!"

"ANGELA! You are totally MAD!" said Laura in admiration. "Wait till I tell Maisie about this!"

Chapter 2

"MUD?" said Maisie in disbelief.

Laura nodded. "She ate the mud sandwich."

They were standing in the playground, waiting for the bell to go.

"What did it taste like?" Maisie asked.

"Muddy," said Angela, screwing up her nose.

"But you didn't actually *swallow* it?" said Maisie.

"Only a little bit," said Angela.

Maisie pulled a face. "YUCK! You'll be sick, Angela! People *die* of eating mud, you know!"

Angela rolled her eyes. It was only some mud, after all. She bet Bertie, the boy next door, had eaten mud. He'd probably eaten worse things, too – like slugs or snails or school rice pudding.

In any case, Angela thought, it had shut up the Ugly Sisters. They hadn't expected her to actually go through with it.

Maisie shook her head. "You are barmy bonkers, Angela," she said.

Angela shrugged. "The point is, what about next time?"

"Next time?" said Laura.

"Of course! You don't think they'll leave us alone?" said Angela. "I bet you they'll be waiting for us again tomorrow."

Laura hadn't thought of that. The Payne twins were like nits – it was very difficult to get rid of them.

"You could tell Miss Darling," suggested Maisie.

"What can *she* do?" asked Angela.

"Tell them off," said Maisie.

Angela shook her head. The twins got told off fifty times a day. They just scowled and took no notice.

"We could walk to school another way," suggested Laura.

"Why *should* we?" cried Angela. "It's not *their* alley. No, we'll just have to stand up to them."

Laura stared. "Are you joking?"

"There are three of us," Angela pointed out.

"Oh no, count me out," said Maisie. "It's not me they're after."

Angela sighed. What happened to friends sticking together? But there had to be *something* they could do. She wasn't eating mud sandwiches for the rest of her life.

"We'll just have to run for it," she said. "You've seen the twins in PE – they couldn't catch a cold."

Laura looked doubtful. Was that the best idea Angela could come up with? She hoped Eileen and Myleen wouldn't be waiting at the alley tomorrow. Maybe by then they'd have forgotten the whole thing. But somehow it didn't seem very likely.

Chapter 3

Next morning, Angela woke up with
a sick feeling in her stomach. For a
moment she thought she'd eaten too
much trifle, then she remembered –
the twins…

She and Laura set off early, hoping to
beat the enemy. But when they turned the
corner, there were the twins, ugly as ever.

"What shall we do?" wailed Laura.

"Pretend you haven't seen them," whispered Angela.

"I think they *saw* me see them!" said Laura.

"Just keep walking," muttered Angela, "and get ready to run."

The twins were leaning against the wall just inside the alley.

Angela took a deep breath. "GO!" she yelled.

They raced into the alley, with their heads down. The twins stepped out to cut them off. Laura dodged between them as Angela swerved round Myleen. Angela heard a thump but she kept running till they were both safely past.

"OH, GOLDILOCKS!" sang Myleen. "Look what I've got!"

Angela turned round. Myleen was holding up her school bag. It must have fallen off her shoulder as she raced past. Her mum would go bananas if she came home without it. She groaned, and walked back to the twins.

Myleen was picking over her lunch. "Carrot sticks? EWW!"

"We'll just have the crisps and chocolate," sniggered Eileen.

"Hands off," said Angela.

"Ooh, I'm scared," said Eileen.

"If Miss Darling finds out, you're in big trouble," said Laura.

"Yeah? Who's going to tell her?" sneered Myleen.

Laura didn't answer.

Eileen took a drink from Angela's bottle and wiped her mouth. "Fizzy orange. Want some, Myleen?"

"Don't mind if I do."

GLUG, GLUG, GLUG!

Myleen tipped back the bottle. "Oh dear, all gone!" she said.

"Poor little Goldilocks," said Eileen.

Myleen looked around and noticed a large muddy puddle by the wall. Going over, she filled the bottle with filthy brown water and thick sludge, then shook it up to make a murky potion.

"Look, Angela, a nice drink for *you*." Myleen held out the bottle.

Angela glared. "I'm not thirsty."

"Aww, go on, try it," said Eileen.

Laura caught Angela's eye and shook her head.

"She's chicken," jeered Myleen. "CLUCK, CLUCK, CLUCK!"

Angela snatched the bottle and took a big gulp. "BLECH!" She spat out the water on the ground.

"HA! HA! HA!" hooted the twins.

Angela stomped off down the alley, her cheeks burning.

"See you tomorrow, Goldilocks!" Myleen called after her.

Angela wiped her mouth. "Right, that's it," she muttered. "I'll get them for this."

"Yeah," said Laura. "Let's call them names like – like – 'silly sausage'."

Angela sighed. Would she gain revenge by calling the twins "silly sausage"? No. She wanted to teach those bullies a lesson. But how? Myleen and Eileen were bigger and meaner than anyone in their class. *But wait*, thought Angela, *there are* other *classes*. She smiled. She knew just the person to talk to.

Chapter 4

DING DONG!

Angela reached up and rang next door's bell. Bertie's mum answered.

"Oh, Angela!" she said. "Bertie's still getting dressed I'm afraid."

"That's okay – is Suzy there?" asked Angela.

"Suzy!"

Angela and Laura exchanged looks as Bertie's mum called up. Footsteps clumped downstairs and Suzy appeared. She was Bertie's older sister and almost in the top year. In Angela's eyes she was practically a giant.

"Hi, Suzy," smiled Angela.

"Hey, Angela, what's up?"

"Can we carry your bag to school?"

Suzy laughed. "Why?"

Angela shrugged. "We'd like to!" she said.

"We like carrying things," added Laura.

Suzy shook her head. Little kids were funny. Still, it would be quite nice having a couple of servants to carry her stuff. She could get used to this.

"Suits me," she said, handing over the bag. "Don't drop it though. It's got my lunch in it."

"We won't," promised Angela. "When are you leaving?"

Suzy glanced at her watch. "Five minutes," she said. "I'll meet you in the playground."

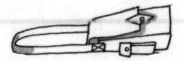

Angela and Laura set off. Angela swung Suzy's bag on to her shoulder. Her lunch was hidden in Laura's rucksack.

"I still don't see how this will work," sighed Laura.

"You'll see," said Angela. "Leave it to me."

They turned the corner and came in sight of the alley. Sure enough, the Payne twins were waiting for them.

Angela walked right up to them, wearing a big cheesy grin.

"What's up with you?" scowled Myleen.

"Nothing. What's up with you?" said Angela.

She tried to walk past, but Eileen

stuck out her hand. "You never learn, do you?" she said. "No payment, no entry."

Myleen noticed the bag on Angela's shoulder. "Is that new?"

Angela nodded. "Yes, but you better not touch it," she warned.

"Or what?" said Myleen. "You'll run crying to your mummy?"

"Heh, heh! Your mummy!" sniggered Eileen.

"Hand it over," ordered Myleen.

Angela sighed heavily. She'd tried to warn them. Myleen reached into the bag and brought out a pink lunch box.

"But that's not ... OW!" cried Laura as Angela stepped on her foot.

Myleen was eyeing the goodies in the lunch box.

"Choccie chunk cookies," she said. "Yum!"

"And cheesy puffs," said Eileen. "Double yum."

They crammed their mouths full, slurping noisily.

Angela glanced back over her shoulder. *Any moment now*, she thought. *Here she comes, right on time...*

"HEY, BIG NOSE! THAT'S MY BAG!" yelled an angry voice.

Suzy was marching towards them. She towered over the twins, grim-faced.

"Y-y-your bag?" stammered Myleen.

"YES, MINE," snapped Suzy. "And that's my lunch you're scoffing, too!"

Myleen wiped the crumbs from her mouth. Eileen had turned pale.

"But Angela was carrying it," she croaked.

"That's right, I said she could," nodded Suzy. She turned to Angela and Laura. "Have these two creeps been bothering you?"

Angela nodded. "They took my crisps," she said.

"And they made her eat mud!" added Laura.

"Did they now?" said Suzy. She glared at the twins, who seemed to be shrinking by the minute.

"It was only a joke," mumbled Myleen.

"Yeah, we were just messing about," gulped Eileen.

"So you like jokes?" said Suzy. "Well, here's one for you."

She turned over a stone with her foot. Earwigs slithered in the dirt.

95

"Worm pie," smiled Suzy. "Who'd like to try it first?"

Myleen gasped. "You're n-not serious?"

"Oh, very serious," nodded Suzy.

The twins had both gone white. They let out a shriek of terror and fled down the alley.

Angela smiled. Somehow she didn't think the terrible twins would be bothering her for quite some time.